Happy Silly Birthday to Me

by Ann McGovern
Illustrated by Sue Dreamer

Cartwheel
B·O·O·K·S ™

SCHOLASTIC INC.
New York London Toronto Sydney Auckland

*For Christopher Mulligan, who inspired this book
when he visited his newborn brother, Dennis,
in the hospital and decided to have his
third birthday party in an elevator.*
—A.M.

To my 2-year-old daughter, Lily
—S.D.

ISBN 0-590-46365-9

12 11 10 9 8 7 6 5 4 3 2 1   4 5 6 7 8 9/10

Printed in the U.S.A.   24

First Scholastic printing, March 1994

When I go to sleep
In my cozy bed,
Silly birthday parties
Dance in my head.

In an elevator in my town,
I go up, up, up; I go down, down, down.
I press a button for my floor;
I press another to open the door.
Happy up-and-down birthday to me!

At my party on a pirate ship,
Will we find treasure on this trip?
I wear a patch over one eye;
I hold my parrot way up high.

Happy yo-ho-ho birthday to me!

Maybe my party will be with the clowns.
The ladies on elephants wear fancy crowns;
Here come the acrobat circus bears
Tumbling down a flight of stairs.
Happy cotton-candy birthday to me!

Oooh! A birthday party with goblins and ghosts!
We eat rat-tail soup and ghastly green toast.
I climb upon the witch's broom
And fly around the scary room.
Happy frighty-night birthday to me!

In a rocket to the moon!
Hurry! Will we be there soon?
We'll travel among the twinkling stars;
Maybe we'll stop awhile on Mars.
Happy out-in-space birthday to me!

A birthday party under the sea!
I dive down deep. I feel so free.
Among the sharks and colorful fishes
Are pretty mermaids blowing kisses.
Happy fishy-wishy birthday to me!

A party in a hot-air balloon!
I soar to the sky on a warm day in June.
I fly over hills till I get to my town.
Ever so gently, the balloon puts me down.
Happy high-in-the-sky birthday to me!

All aboard my birthday train!
We'll start in California. We'll end up in Maine!
I pull a cord and the whistle wails
As we go *choo-choo-chooing* down the rails.
Happy *clickety-clackety* birthday to me!

At my birthday party on a jungle floor,
I see TWO snakes, THREE snakes, FOUR snakes, MORE!
I hear a monkey howl; I hear an owl hoot.
A purple snake slithers out of my boot!
Happy jungly-mungly birthday to me!

There's a birthday party in the firehouse!
With a fire dog and a fire mouse
And hoses and hats and rubber boots
And sirens that wail and a horn that toots.
Happy fire-engine birthday to me!

And a birthday party in an orchestra.
With a *tee-dee-dee-dee* and a *tra-la-la-la*
And a big brass horn and a fine set of drums.
Everybody sings; everybody hums.
Happy *boom-de-boom* birthday to me!

My party will be on a wide, white beach;
The ocean waves are just out of reach.
We make sandy cakes all in rows —
The sea comes in and kisses my toes.
Happy sandy-dandy birthday to me!

At my party in the city zoo,
I'll share a toy with a kangaroo.
The panda and monkeys sing me a song;
My party will last the whole day long.
Happy zooey-zoo birthday to me!

When I go to sleep
In my cozy bed,
Silly birthday parties
Dance in my head.

In an elevator, on a pirate ship,
In a circus, on a ghostly trip;
In a rocket to the moon,
Under the sea, up in a balloon;
On a train crisscrossing the land —
In a jungle, a firehouse, a band;
On the beach, and in the zoo,
Happy silly birthday to me!
Happy silly birthday to you!

Giraffe Trouble

by Jean Craighead George

Illustrated by Anna Vojtech

Disney PRESS

New York

A lioness roared from the lake shore when Cam was born.

The calf's stately mother paid no attention. She was a big and powerful giraffe. She could protect Cam with her long legs and sharp hooves. She could knock down a lion or a hyena.

And she was protected by friends. Four alert mother giraffes were in the woods guarding the giraffe nursery where their calves and Cam lay. The mothers watched for lions and hyenas, cheetahs and angry hippos. When they went out to browse, the giraffe fathers stood guard.

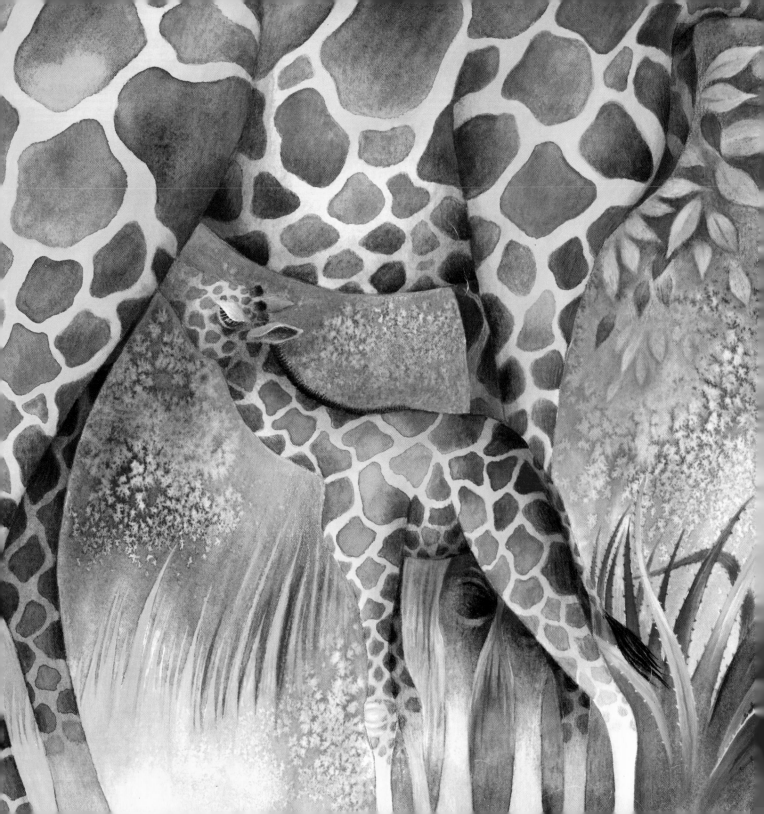

Cam was six feet tall at birth. No sooner had her mother licked her dry with her eighteen-inch-long tongue than Cam got to her feet and nursed. A few hours later she stepped out of the nursery to look at the world. Cam was utterly fearless. This worried her mother. Fearless calves often do not grow up. They need to be wise as well.

It was early morning when Cam stepped out onto the savanna. The rainy season had just begun. The grasses were a fresh spring-green. Herds of zebras, gazelles, and wildebeests grazed all the way to the mountains. Thousands of them fed on the grasses.

Not her family. The long-necked giraffes found their meals high above everyone else. They relished the leaves of the trees. The big bulls could reach up more than nineteen feet.

Cam's family wandered in a loose herd from woodland to woodland. They had no special territory. Adults and young all moved along amicably, finding their own trees and keeping several giraffe lengths apart. Old bulls, like Cam's grandfather Elo, preferred to live alone.

Giraffes are sweet and peaceful animals. They are also very smart. They see trouble and avoid it. Cam's herd drank at the rhino wallow, not the lake where the lions lived. Lions attack young giraffes.

Fortunately, after she had seen the vast savanna, fearless Cam stayed close to her mother. At least she did so for three months. Then she developed a craving for the buds of the combretum trees that grew along the lake.

One day when her mother was eating acacia leaves, Cam smelled the tasty combretum. Fearlessly she strode off to find them. She walked past the lion pride. The lioness opened one eye. She did not stalk Cam. Even a little giraffe can kick hard. She would wait until Cam lay down to chew her cud and rest.

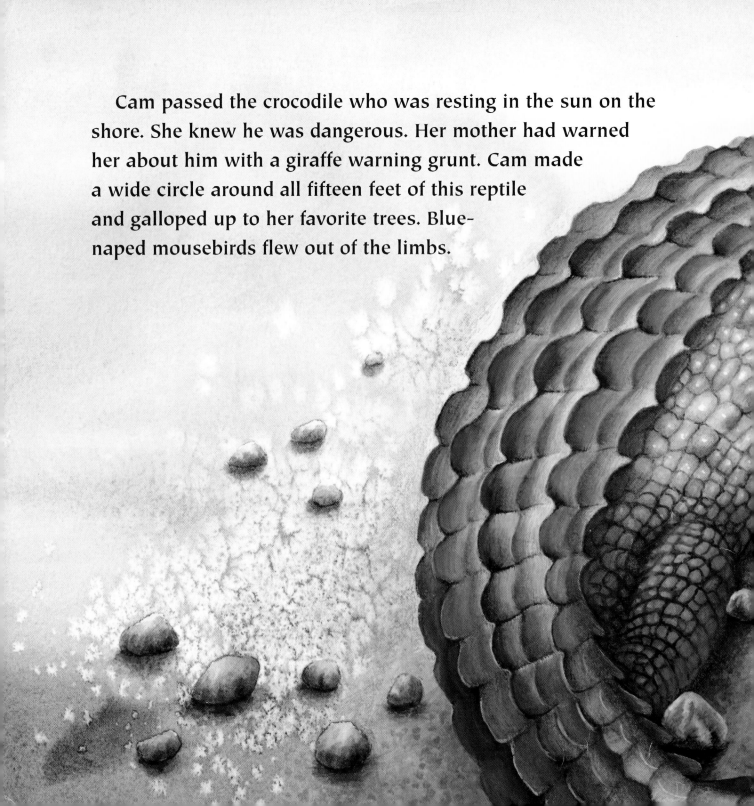

Cam passed the crocodile who was resting in the sun on the shore. She knew he was dangerous. Her mother had warned her about him with a giraffe warning grunt. Cam made a wide circle around all fifteen feet of this reptile and galloped up to her favorite trees. Blue-naped mousebirds flew out of the limbs.

She lifted her long muzzle into the tasty leaves
and tore them off with her flexible upper lip. Her
long tongue reached out and whipped the leaves
into her mouth. She ate and ate.

When she was stuffed, she walked to a patch of
grass. Cam got down on her front knees, then her
back knees, and finally rolled comfortably onto
her side. She lay perfectly still. The croc did not
see her, for crocs see only things that move.

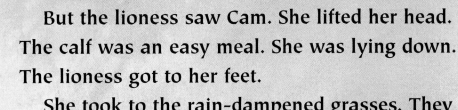

But the lioness saw Cam. She lifted her head. The calf was an easy meal. She was lying down. The lioness got to her feet.

She took to the rain-dampened grasses. They did not rustle when she walked through them like dry grasses do. In utter silence, she stalked Cam.

Along the lake lived a community of sharp-eyed birds. The flamingos saw the lioness. As one, they all stopped swinging their beaks in the muddy backwater and stretched up their necks.

"*Ka-baunk.*" They screamed out the flamingo alarm cry. Cam opened her eyes.

The cry alerted the ducks. They, too, saw the lioness, honked, and took to the air. Cam lifted her long neck and head.

The ducks alerted a flock of Egyptian geese. Wind from their big wings bent the grasses. As they flew off, Cam saw the lioness.

It took mere seconds to lift her rear end, get to her front knees, and stand up. That was too long. The lioness was in the air coming toward her like a missile.

Out of nowhere came Elo, the old bull giraffe. He slashed down on the lioness with his razor-sharp hooves. The lioness rolled into the dust, gained her feet, and sped away. The old bull sounded the raucous cough of the victorious male.

Cam galloped back to the nursery. Her mother greeted her by curling her long lip over Cam's nose. She did not scold Cam. Wise youngsters of the wild learn from mistakes.

Cam was now both fearless and wise. Her mother gently rubbed her head against Cam's. Her calf would grow up after all.

Cast of Characters

RETICULATED GIRAFFE
Cam
scientific name: *Giraffa camelopardalis reticulata*

The giraffe is the tallest mammal in the world, easily recognized by its long, long legs and neck. When they are three years old, males leave their mothers and join bachelor herds. The males have a medium horn and four or more bumps for fighting contests. One young is born after a gestation of fourteen to fifteen months.

LION
King of the African Carnivores
Cam's enemy
scientific name: *Panthera leo*

A large robust cat with smooth tawny coat and a long tail with a black tassel at tip. The male develops a blond, tawny, or even black mane in his third year. One to four, rarely five or six, cubs are born after a 3.5-month gestation. The cubs have brownish spots that fade around three months of age.

LONG-SNOUTED CROCODILE
Cam's lake edge enemy
scientific name: *Crocodylus cataphractus*

Crocodiles are large, lizardlike animals with powerful jaws, many teeth, short legs, and webbed toes. The ancestors of the crocodile lived at the same time as the dinosaurs. Of the world's twenty-three species, most are endangered. They eat fish, but will ambush antelopes, buffaloes, zebras, and domestic animals that come to their waterways to drink. They lay thirteen to twenty-seven eggs in a mound of vegetable debris, which warms the eggs as it decays.

EGYPTIAN GOOSE
Cam's water friend
scientific name: *Alopochen aegyptacus*

This large, pale gray and brown goose with white shoulders wears dark rings around its eyes. No other large waterfowl has these. It mates for life and nests on the ground or in tree holes.

FLAMINGO
Cam's friend who warns her of danger
scientific name: *Phoenicopterus ruber*

The flamingo is a huge, white or pale pink bird with a long S-shaped neck. It builds a tall mud nest in which it makes a depression for one egg. When feeding it walks steadily in water keeping its head submerged for up to twenty-five seconds. It stirs up the bottom mud with its feet and filters out tiny water life from the mud.

ZEBRA
Cam's savanna neighbor
scientific name: *Equus burchelli*

The zebra resembles a sturdy pony, decorated with handsome black or brown stripes that distinguish it from all other beasts. A male weighs about 550 pounds, the female about 480. Females give birth to one foal after a twelve month gestation.

WILDEBEEST
Brindled Gnu
Cam's savanna neighbor
scientific name: *Connochaetes taurinus*

A wildebeest is an unusual-looking antelope with flat muzzle, cow-like horns, and short neck. It is blue-gray or brown. It weighs 350 to 600 pounds. One calf is born after a gestation of eight to eight-and-a-half months. It migrates in huge herds on the savanna.

Disney is committed to wildlife conservation worldwide. At Disney's Animal Kingdom, most of the animals that guests will see were born in zoological parks. A safari adventure ride features live animals in a re-creation of the African savanna. Guests can also visit Conservation Station, the headquarters for conservation and species survival activities.

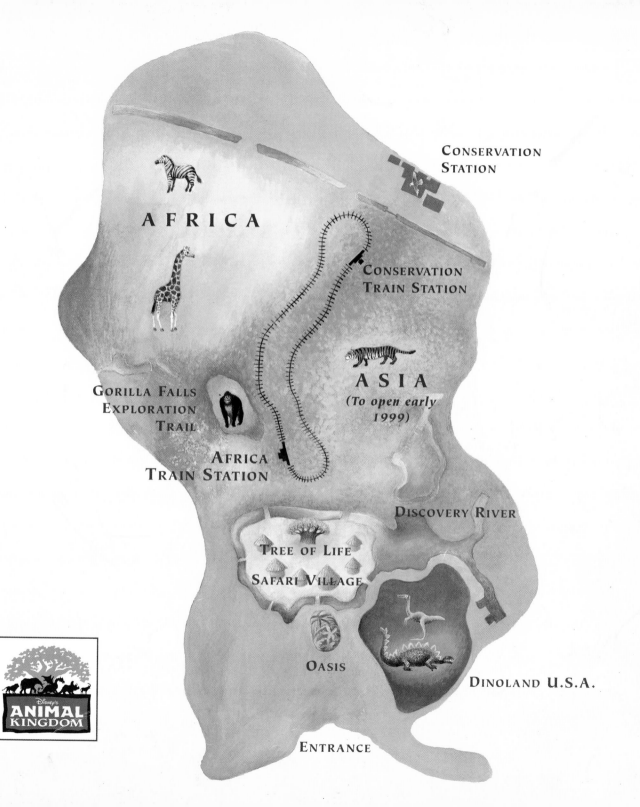

CONSERVATION
STATION

AFRICA

CONSERVATION
TRAIN STATION

ASIA
*(To open early
1999)*

GORILLA FALLS
EXPLORATION
TRAIL

AFRICA
TRAIN STATION

DISCOVERY RIVER

TREE OF LIFE

SAFARI VILLAGE

OASIS

DINOLAND U.S.A.

DISNEP'S
ANIMAL
KINGDOM

ENTRANCE

To Kate
—J.C.G.

To Franciska and Johanna
—A.V.

Printed in the United States of America.
The text for this book is set in 16-point Tiepolo Bold. The artwork for
each picture was painted with watercolors.

First Edition
1 3 5 7 9 10 8 6 4 2

Library of Congress Cataloging-in-Publication Data
George, Jean Craighead, (date)
Giraffe trouble / by Jean Craighead George; illustrated by Anna Vojtech.
—1st ed.
p.   cm.
Summary: A young giraffe living on the African plains learns how to be
wise as well as fearless when a lion attacks.
ISBN 0-7868-3167-7 (trade)—0-7868-5066-3 (lib. bdg.)
1. Giraffe—Juvenile fiction.   [1. Giraffe—Fiction.]
I. Vojtech, Anna, ill.   II. Title.
PZ10.3.G316Gi   1998
[E]—dc21   97-33130